Usborne

Little
Children's Book
of Things to Do

Fiona Watt

Illustrated by Katie Lovell

Photographs by Howard Allman
Digital manipulation by Nick Wakeford

Farm

Fluffy lamb

1. Draw a big oval for a lamb's body.

2. Fingerpaint a black head. Then, fingerprint ears.

3. Fingerpaint four long legs. Leave the paint to dry.

4. Pull cotton balls into pieces, then roll them into balls.

5. Spread glue on the body and press on the cotton balls.

6. Glue another little cotton ball onto the head.

Muddy pigs

1. Dip your finger in pink paint and go around and around for an oval body.

2. Mix darker pink paint and fingerpaint a nose and legs.

3. Fingerpaint lots of brown mud around the pig and on its body.

4. When the paint is dry, draw a face, ears and a curly tail.

Tractor

1. Cut a rectangle from paper. Glue it onto another piece of paper.

2. Cut out a square for the cab and glue it on top, like this.

Use a black crayon.

3. Draw a big wheel at the back and a small one at the front.

4. Draw a window on the cab. Draw a funnel and some curly smoke.

5. Draw some long muddy tracks under the tractor.

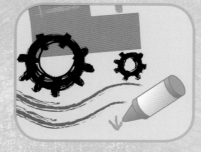

6. Draw clumps of grass around the tracks.

9

Chirpy chicks

1. Draw a circle with yellow chalk for a chick's body and fill it in.

2. Smudge the chalk around and around with your finger, to make a fluffy shape.

Add an eye, too.

3. Draw a beak, a wing and legs with an orange pencil.

4. Draw lots of little lines around your chick for feathers.

You could draw
lots of little
chicks together.

Printed cows

Leave
the
paint
to dry.

1. Cut a small square of sponge. Then, pour some black paint on an old plate.

2. Dip the sponge in the paint and print squares all over a piece of white paper.

3. Cut a body and head from the printed paper. Glue them onto a piece of paper.

4. Draw four legs and two ears. Cut them out and glue them on.

5. Use a pink pencil to fill in the cow's nose. Draw two eyes and a tail.

Hens

1. Cut a half circle from a piece of patterned paper, for a hen's body.

2. Glue it onto a piece of paper, with the straight edge at the top.

Draw a black dot for an eye.

3. Cut a triangle for a beak from a different piece of paper and glue it beside the body.

4. Use bright chalks to draw legs and a wing. Add feathers on the head and tail.

You could cut
a henhouse
from patterned
paper, too.

15

Hay barn

1. Draw a barn and cut it out. Glue it onto a piece of paper.

2. Cut strips for the roof and cut out a window. Glue them on.

Lay the strips like this.

3. Cut two strips of sponge cloth, making one wider than the other.

4. Roll the strips together and secure them with sticky tape.

5. Spread yellow paint on an old plate. Dip the sponge into it.

6. Print lots of bales of hay inside the barn. Then, let it dry.

Happy horse

1. Paint a rectangle for a horse's body.

2. Paint a neck and a head. Add little ears.

3. Add four long legs beneath the body.

Draw with the
end of a brush.

4. Mix a paler shade
of brown and paint
a nose and hooves.

5. Paint a tail and
mane. Draw lines
into the wet paint.

6. When the paint
is dry, draw an eye,
nose and mouth.

19

Hairy goat

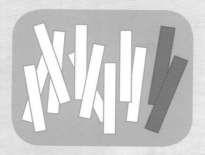

1. Cut thin strips of white paper, and two brown strips.

2. Roll the strips into coils, then put them aside.

3. Mix light brown paint with lots of thick white glue.

Spread the paint on thickly.

4. Paint a rectangle for a body. Add a neck, head and ear.

5. Paint four thin legs with darker hooves. Add a little tail.

6. While the paint is wet, press the white coils onto the body.

7. Unroll the ends of the brown coils. Dip one edge into glue.

8. Then, press the coils onto the head as horns, like this.

9. Paint a nose, and the inside of the ear. Draw an eye and a mouth.

Farmyard ducks

1. Draw a shape for a duck's body with a wax crayon.

2. Draw an orange beak, an eye and a little wing.

3. Fill in the body. Press firmly as you do it.

4. Draw blue lines below the body and add reeds.

5. Mix lots of watery blue paint. Brush the paint over the bottom of the duck and reeds, for a pond.

23

Scarecrow

1. Use crayons to draw a little hill, and a stick for the scarecrow.

2. Cut a 'T' shape from paper or fabric. Glue it on top of the stick.

3. Cut a circle for the scarecrow's head and glue it on, too.

4. Snip little pieces of string. Glue them onto the head and arms.

5. Cut out a big brown hat and glue it on top of the hair.

6. Draw a face with pencils. Glue some old buttons on his coat.

Fieldmice

Let the
paint dry.

1. Draw long
stems of wheat
with a yellow
wax crayon.

2. Dip your finger
into some paint
and print a
mouse's body.

3. Use pencils
to draw an eye,
ears, a nose, feet
and a tail.

Print lots of mice running up
and down the stems.

Easter

Spring lambs

1. Draw a circle for a lamb's body with pink or lilac chalk and fill it in.

2. Draw a head, ears and four legs with a dark pencil. Add eyes and a nose.

3. Fill the head, ears and legs with purple chalk. Smudge the chalk a little with your finger.

4. Use white chalk to draw around and around on the lamb's back for fluffy wool.

Easter egg tag

1. Draw an egg on a small piece of thin cardboard.

2. Turn the cardboard over and paint it. Let the paint dry.

Lay the strips like this.

3. Cut small strips of ribbon and glue them onto the cardboard.

4. When the glue is dry, turn the cardboard over. Cut out the egg.

5. Glue on more decorations, such as buttons or sequins.

Use a hole puncher.

6. Punch a hole in the egg and thread some ribbon through.

You could draw stripes with a pencil.

You could fingerprint spots.

This egg had glitter sprinkled on while the paint was still wet.

Bunny card

Don't cut the fold.

1. Fold a rectangle of thin cardboard in half. Draw a shape for a body against the fold, like this.

2. Draw a shape for a head on another piece of cardboard. Add two long ears.

3. Cut around the shapes. Then, put the piece for the body to the side.

Pull the legs apart
to make the card stand up.

Let the
glue dry.

4. Cut shapes for a nose, cheeks and ears from pieces of material. Glue them onto the head.

5. When the glue is dry, draw two eyes and a little mouth with a pen.

6. Glue the head onto the body. Then, glue on a piece of a cotton ball, for a tail.

Butterfly garland

Let the glue dry.

1. Cut two rectangles of patterned paper and glue them back to back.

2. Fold the paper in half and draw a butterfly wing against the fold.

Don't cut here.

3. Holding the paper together, carefully cut out the wing.

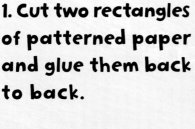

4. Open out the wings. Then, cut two strips from thick paper for the body.

Let the glue dry.

5. Glue the strips onto the wings, one on either side, to make the body.

6. Use a hole puncher to make holes in the body, one in either end.

Glue them here.

7. Glue on two smaller strips of paper for feelers.

8. Use different scraps of patterned paper to make more butterflies.

9. Thread a long piece of string through the holes to make a garland.

35

Hen collage

Let the paint dry.

1. Paint lots of spots on one piece of paper and stripes on another one.

2. Draw a shape for a hen on the spotted paper. Cut it out and glue it onto a piece of thick paper.

3. Draw a wing and some tail feathers on the striped paper. Cut them out.

36

To make a nest,
glue strips of paper
overlapping each other.
Then, cut out eggs and
glue them on top.

4. Draw a beak,
legs and feathers
for the head on
some plain paper.
Cut them out, too.

5. Glue all the
pieces onto the
hen. Then, use
a pen to draw
an eye.

6. Cut some
strips of paper
for grass and
glue them
around the hen.

Printed chick

Print some wings, too.

1. Cut a triangle from a piece of sponge. Then, pour yellow paint onto an old plate.

2. Dip the sponge into the paint, then press it onto a piece of thick paper.

3. Press it onto the paper again and again to make a circle for the chick's body.

Trim the ends of the feet a little.

4. Cut a beak from some orange material. Then, cut two pieces of pipe cleaner.

5. Twist one piece around the other to make a foot. Make another foot in the same way.

6. Glue the beak and legs onto the body. Then, draw two little dots for eyes.

Springtime tree

1. Paint a tree trunk with pale pink paint on thick paper.

2. Using pale green paint, add an oval at the top of the trunk and fill it in.

Let the paint dry.

3. Use a thinner brush to paint some little leaves and grass, too.

4. Mix watery pink, green and white paints on an old plate.

5. Dip your finger in the paints and print lots of little dots for flowers.

The smaller dots on this tree were printed with the end of a paintbrush.

Easter basket

1. Draw a basket and a handle on a piece of light brown paper.

2. Draw lots of lines across the basket with a brown pencil.

3. Cut out the shapes. Glue them onto another piece of paper.

4. Cut a flower from a piece of material. Glue it onto the basket.

5. Cut a circle from another piece of material and glue it on.

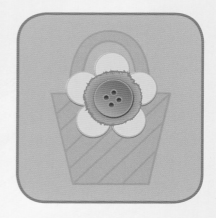

6. Glue on an old button for the middle of the flower.

You could glue
a basket onto
the front of an
Easter card.

Try making lots of
different shapes
of baskets.

This basket has
eggs cut from
material. The
basket was glued
on top of them.

Hanging bird

Cut through both layers.

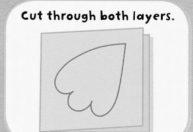

1. Draw half a circle for a bird's body on bright paper. Add a head and a beak.

2. Cut out the bird. Then, erase any pencil lines.

3. Fold another piece of paper in half. Draw a wing and cut it out.

Glue the wings like this.

4. Make a hole in the bird's back using a hole puncher.

5. Push some thread through the hole for hanging.

6. Spread glue along the edge of each wing and press them on.

Crocus cards

1. Draw a flower with three petals on a piece of thick purple paper. Cut it out.

2. Carefully fold down the middle of each petal, along the dotted lines shown here.

3. Then, make a fold between each petal to make a shape, like this.

This card had a piece of patterned paper glued on first.

You could glue several crocuses onto one card.

Keep the paper folded as you cut.

These will be the stamens.

4. Fold a long piece of green paper in half and cut a thin leaf against the fold.

5. Cut a stem from green paper. Cut three small strips from orange paper, too.

6. Fold some paper for a card. Glue on the stem, leaf and stamens. Then, glue the flower on top.

47

Easter bouquet

You need to press quite hard.

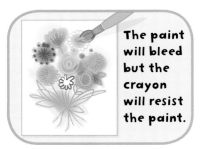

The paint will bleed but the crayon will resist the paint.

1. Using bright wax crayons, draw a bunch of flowers on thick paper.

2. Mix some watery paints in old pots. Brush your picture with clean water.

3. While the paint is wet, paint the leaves and dot bright paint onto each flower.

4. When the paint is dry, draw some more flowers and petals with felt-tip pens.

You could draw different sizes and shapes of flowers.

Dinosaurs

Printed T. rex

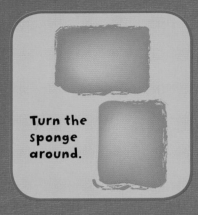

Turn the sponge around.

1. Spread paint on an old plate. Then, dip a sponge into it.

2. Print a body by pressing the sponge onto a piece of paper.

3. Dip the sponge into the paint again and print a head, like this.

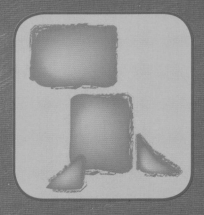

Leave the paint to dry.

4. Cut a corner off the sponge and use it to print a leg and a tail.

5. Fingerpaint two little arms. Then, fingerprint an eye with a pupil, too.

6. Draw a face, claws and spikes on the back with chalk or a crayon.

You could
fingerprint
spots on your
T. rex's body.

Stand-up diplodocus

Leave room for the head and tail.

1. Fold a piece of thick paper in half. Draw a body against the fold.

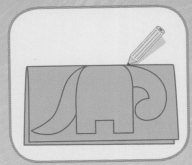

2. Draw a long, thick tail. Add a neck curving down. Then, draw a head, too.

Don't cut along the fold.

3. Carefully cut around the dinosaur. Then, open it out and lay it flat.

Pull the legs apart a little to make your diplodocus stand up.

52

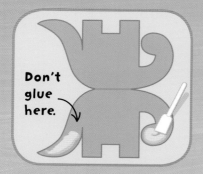

Don't glue here.

4. Spread glue on the tail, neck and head. Fold the shape again and press it together.

Add toenails and a rosy cheek, too.

5. When the glue is dry, erase the lines on the body. Draw nostrils, an eye and a mouth.

6. Then, draw wiggly shapes on the dinosaur's body and fill them in, too.

Stegosaurus

1. Paint a big circle for a body with bright green paint.

2. Paint a neck and head, and two thick legs. Paint a tail, too.

3. When the paint is dry, fingerprint lots of dots on the body and tail.

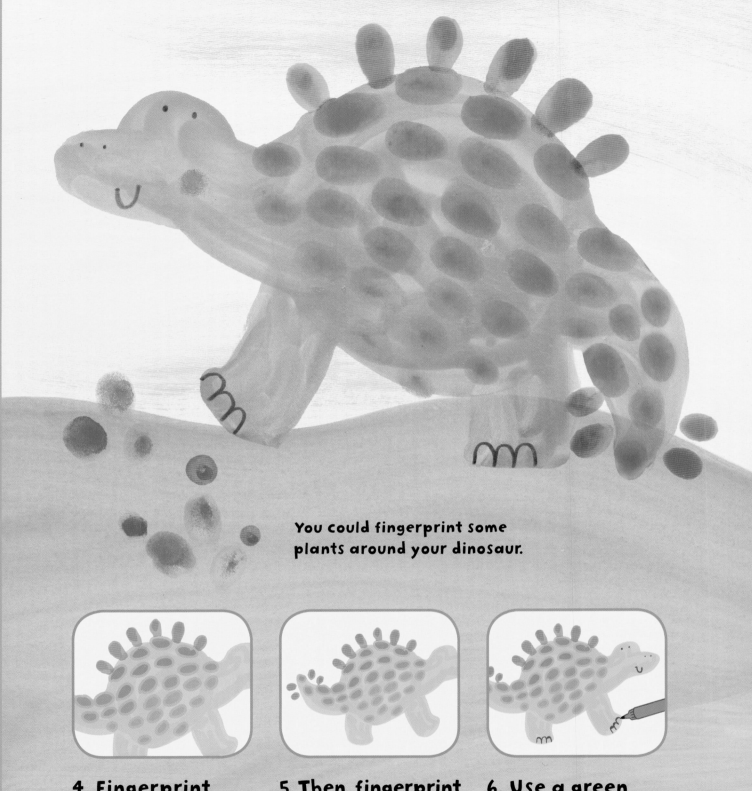

You could fingerprint some plants around your dinosaur.

4. Fingerprint some red spikes along the body, like this.

5. Then, fingerprint two little spikes on either side of the tail.

6. Use a green pen to draw a face. Then, add curved toenails.

Flying pterosaur

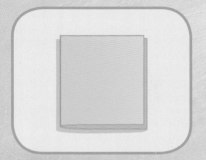

1. Fold a rectangle of thick paper in half.

2. Draw a line across it for the top of the wings.

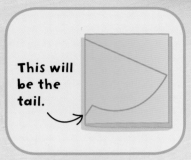

This will be the tail.

3. Draw a curve for the wings, and a line for a tail.

4. Cut along the lines, then unfold the paper.

Draw a mouth, too.

5. Draw a head and cut it out. Then, add an eye.

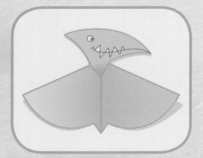

6. Glue or tape the head onto the wings.

7. Draw the body, claws, arms and lines on the wings.

Tape a foot onto each end.

8. Cut out feet and tape them onto some string.

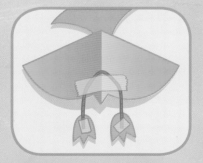

9. Tape the string onto the back of the wings.

To hang up your pterosaur, tape some thread on the back.

You could try making pterosaurs with different sizes of wings.

57

Dinosaur eggs

1. Mix runny paint in an old container. Then, lay a piece of paper on an old newspaper.

Pull your finger across the bristles.

2. Dip a brush into the paint. Use your finger to splatter the paper with paint.

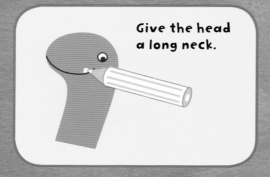

Give the head a long neck.

3. While the paint is drying, cut out a baby dinosaur's head. Then, draw its eye and mouth.

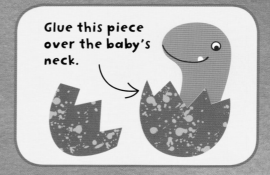

Glue this piece over the baby's neck.

4. Cut an egg from the speckled paper and cut a zigzag across it. Glue the shapes onto some paper.

This egg had glitter
sprinkled onto the
wet paint.

You could splatter
two different paints
onto an egg.

59

Swimming dinosaur

Use a green pen.

1. Draw a body with a felt-tip pen. Add a neck, head and tail.

2. Add four big flippers. Then, draw lots of spots, like this.

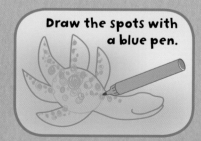

The water will make the ink run.

3. Using a clean paintbrush, brush water all over your drawing.

Draw the spots with a blue pen.

4. When it's dry, draw around the dinosaur again. Add more spots.

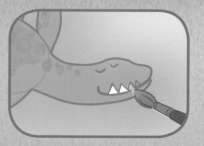

The ink on the spots will run.

5. Carefully brush water inside the dinosaur's body, then let it dry.

6. Use pens to draw a face. Draw some teeth and paint them white.

You could draw
several dinosaurs
swimming together.

Sharp teeth

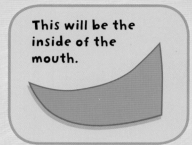

This will be the inside of the mouth.

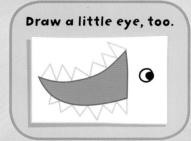

Draw a little eye, too.

1. Draw a shape for a mouth on red or pink paper and cut it out.

2. Glue the mouth onto some white paper. Draw teeth along the edges.

3. Carefully cut around the teeth and mouth. Cut out the eye, too.

You could use these ideas to make other dinosaurs.

Draw scales and nostrils, too.

4. Carefully bend all the teeth over onto the mouth, like this.

5. Draw the top part of a dinosaur on some paper. Fill it with paint.

6. When the paint is dry, glue the mouth and eye onto the dinosaur.

Try drawing different shapes of mouths and teeth.

Spiky ankylosaurus

You could add some claws to your dinosaur.

Leave the paint to dry.

Draw the end of the tail, too.

1. Cut two pieces of cardboard from an old box. Paint one of them.

2. Draw a head, tail and two legs on the plain piece. Cut them out.

3. On the back of the painted cardboard draw a spiky body.

You could bend the
spikes forward to
make them stand up.

Turn the painted
shapes over.

Add a
nostril and
a pupil.

4. Carefully cut
out the shapes.
Then, glue them
together, like this.

5. Cut out more
spikes from plain
cardboard and
glue them on.

6. Cut some teeth
and eyes from
white cardboard
and glue them on.

Triceratops

1. Mix thick paint with some white glue in an old container.

2. Paint a big circle for a body. Add a tail and two legs.

3. Mix slightly paler paint and paint a shape for a head.

Scratch lines into wet paint for patches of grass.

Use the pointed end of a paintbrush.

4. Scratch patterns for scales into the wet paint.

5. Paint horns on the dinosaur's head and scratch lines across them.

6. When the paint is dry, use a felt-tip pen to draw a face.

Apatosaurus

1. Cut lots of leaves and plants from patterned paper or old magazines.

2. Lay them along the bottom edge of a piece of paper. Then, glue them on.

3. Draw some long necks and heads sticking out above the leaves. Draw faces, too.

4. Use chalks to fill in the dinosaurs. Smudge the chalk a little with a finger.

5. Then, glue more leaves around the other edges of your picture.

You could draw
a dinosaur with
its mouth open,
then glue on
some leaves.

69

Plate-o-saurus

1. Cut a paper plate in half. Put one piece for the body, to the side.

Draw the legs against the edge, like this.

2. Draw a tail along the edge of the other piece. Draw two legs, too.

3. Draw a head with a long neck on the flat part of the plate.

You could paint a
background and glue
your dinosaur on top.

Draw a
nostril, too.

4. Cut out the
shapes and tape
them to the back
of the other piece.

5. Turn the
dinosaur over
and paint it. Let
the paint dry.

6. Draw a mouth.
Cut out an eye
and sharp teeth,
then glue them on.

Dinosaur footprints

You need to press quite hard.

The crayon will resist the paint.

1. Using a pale wax crayon, draw an oval for a footprint. Then, fill it in.

2. Draw three small shapes with pointed tips for claws. Fill them in, too.

3. Draw more footprints. Brush watery brown paint over the top of them for mud.

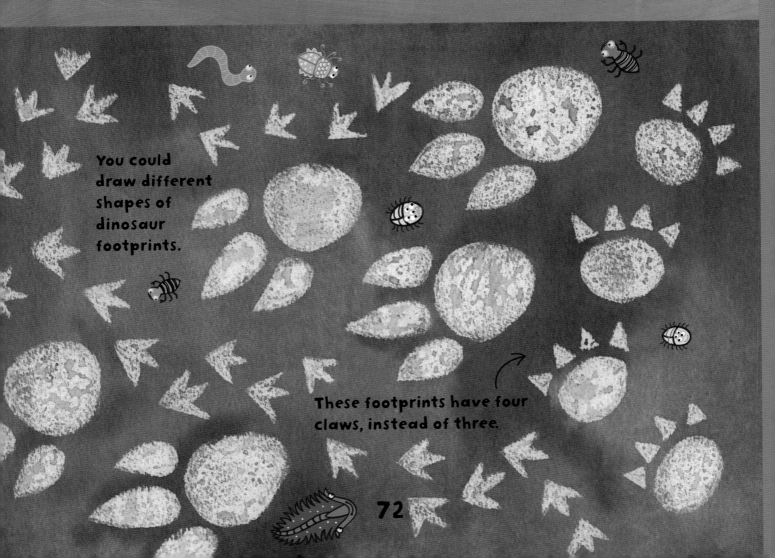

You could draw different shapes of dinosaur footprints.

These footprints have four claws, instead of three.

72

Summer

Salty sea picture

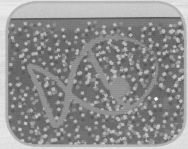

1. Paint a piece of thick blue paper with lots of white glue.

2. Sprinkle the glue with some fine glitter and lots of salt.

3. When the glue is dry, draw a fish with bright pink chalk.

74

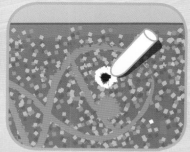

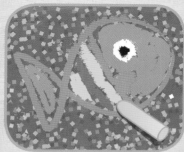

4. Draw a blue eye, then draw around it with white chalk.

5. Then, use red, green and yellow chalks to fill in the fish's body.

6. Draw some big bubbles and seaweed around your fish.

Ice-cream cone

Use light brown paper.

1. Draw around a plate on a piece of paper. Cut out the circle, then cut it in half.

2. Use a brown crayon to draw crisscross lines on the paper, like this.

Hold the cone while the glue dries.

3. Bend the paper around to make a cone shape and glue it in place.

Twist the ends of the paper towel.

4. To make the ice cream, scrunch some paper towels into a ball. Then, wrap another one around the ball.

5. Glue the ball inside the cone. Then, mix some thick paint with white glue in an old container.

Stand the ice cream in a mug until it is dry.

6. Brush the mixture all over the ice cream. Then, sprinkle glitter over the wet paint.

This ice cream had dark pink paint dribbled over it for raspberry sauce.

This ice cream had little beads sprinkled onto it.

You could cut
a flag from
patterned paper
to glue at the top
of the sandcastle.

Printed sandcastle

Use thick paint.

Turn the sponge on its side to print the second rectangle.

Keep the strip for later.

1. Spread some yellow and orange paints on an old plate.

2. Dip a sponge into the yellow paint and print two rectangles.

3. Cut a strip off the end of the sponge, then print a turret.

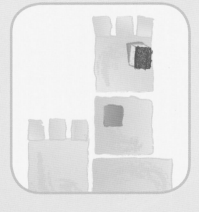

4. Cut the end off the strip and print yellow squares for battlements.

5. Dip the same sponge into the orange paint and print two windows.

6. Print some pale orange squares for decoration. Then, cut a paper door and glue it on.

Kite collage

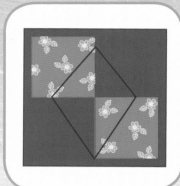

1. Cut two squares of paper. Glue them onto a big square, like this.

2. Draw a kite in the middle of the paper. Then, cut it out.

3. Glue the kite at the top corner of another piece of paper.

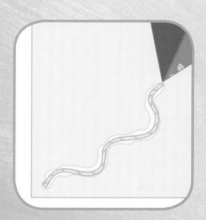

Trim the strips to make them the same size.

4. Cut a piece of string and glue it on in a wiggly line, coming from the bottom of the kite.

5. Cut some thin strips of material and tie a knot in the middle of each one.

6. Trim the ends of the strips, then glue them along the string.

You could decorate
your kite by gluing
on an old button.

You could use paper to make the stem, leaves and petals, if you don't have a pipe cleaner or felt.

Big sunflower

Let the paint dry.

1. Paint the back of two paper plates with red and brown paint.

2. For a stem, glue a pipe cleaner onto a piece of thick paper.

3. Cut the red plate into a pot shape. Glue it over the stem, like this.

4. Cut lots of petals from yellow felt. Cut two green leaves, too.

5. Turn the brown plate over and glue the petals around the edge of the plate.

6. Glue the leaves on either side of the stem. Then, glue the flower on top.

Busy bumble bees

1. Cut an oval for a bee's body from yellow material.

2. Cut two teardrop shapes for wings from silver foil.

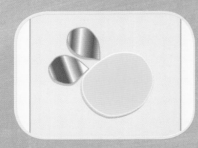

3. Glue the bee's body and wings onto a piece of blue paper, like this.

4. Paint two dark stripes on the body. Then, add eyes, legs and antennae, too.

5. Glue some old beads onto the antennae. Then, use pens to draw a happy face.

You could use paper instead of material for the bee's body.

If you don't have any beads, you could glue on buttons or balls of silver foil.

Happy crab

You could paint a sandy background for your crab.

1. Draw an oval for a crab's body with an orange crayon.

2. Draw two shapes like this, on top of the body for the eyes.

3. Then, draw two large claws beside the eyes. Add some lines on the claws.

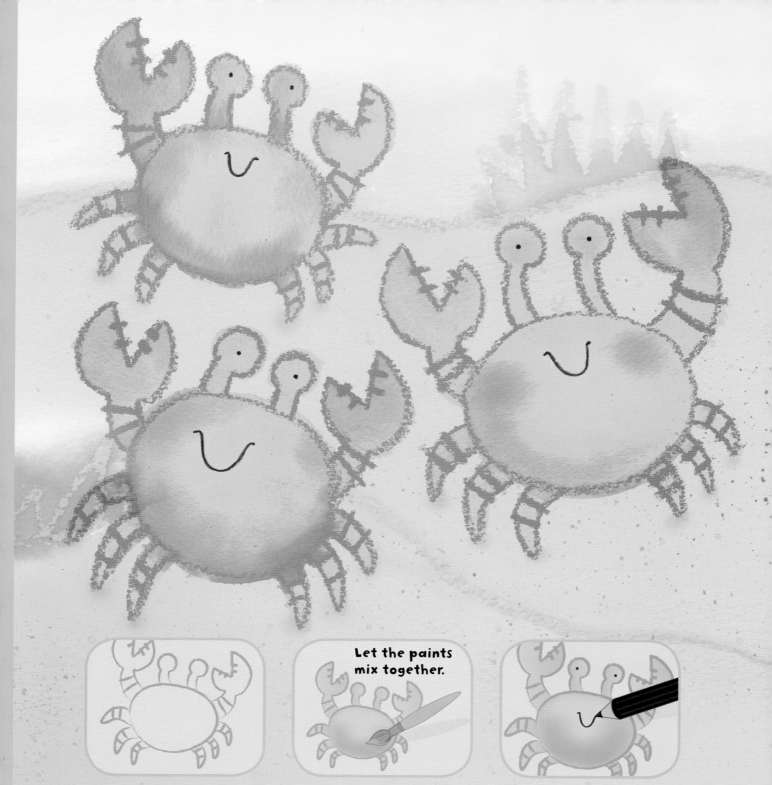

Let the paints
mix together.

4. Add some little legs below the body, and draw lines on them, too.

5. Fill in the crab with watery orange and pink paints.

6. When the paint is dry, draw little dots for eyes and add a smiling mouth.

87

Sparkly Shell

1. Paint a piece of paper with white glue. Let it dry.

2. Mix some thick bright paint with some more glue.

3. Quickly paint a shell shape on the paper.

4. Use the end of the brush to scratch lines into the wet paint.

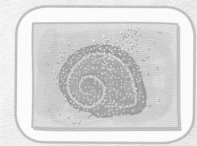

5. Sprinkle the shell with fine glitter. Shake off any extra glitter when the paint is dry.

Use the ideas on these pages for different shapes of shells.

To make a pearl, sprinkle a blob of glue with glitter. Let it dry, then cut it out and glue it on.

Beach hut hanging

Use a hole puncher.

1. Cut a piece of white cardboard and punch holes in the top corners.

2. Use a sponge to print a patch of yellow paint on the cardboard.

3. Cut three shapes for huts from different bright papers.

Cut a little window, too.

4. Cut triangles and strips for the roofs, and some little rectangles for doors.

Leave the glue to dry.

5. Cut a circle for a sun. Then, glue all the shapes onto the cardboard.

6. Tie thick string through the holes, like this, for hanging your picture.

You could make another picture
and tie it below, like this.

Paper boat

You could make a pirate to put in your boat.

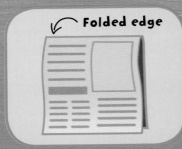

↙ Folded edge

1. Cut a rectangle from an old newspaper and fold it in half.

2. Fold the top corners down so that they meet in the middle.

3. Then, fold up the top layer of the paper at the bottom, like this.

This boat had a paper flag and portholes glued on.

4. Turn the paper over and fold up the paper at the bottom, again.

5. Then, fold both bottom corners up like this, and secure them with tape.

6. Turn the paper over to see your boat with its sail.

strawberries

You could draw some insects hiding in the leaves.

Add some grass, too.

1. Paint several stems, like these, on a piece of thick paper.

2. Paint some soil along the bottom of the paper. Leave it to dry.

3. Draw a shape for a strawberry on red paper. Add dots for seeds.

You could add white strawberries that aren't ripe yet.

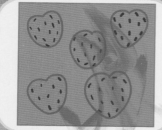

4. Draw more strawberries in the same way and cut them out.

5. Cut out some green leaves using paper from old magazines.

6. Glue a strawberry onto the end of each stem. Glue the leaves on, too.

Summer sandals

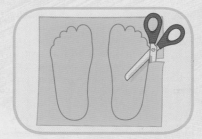

1. Draw around your feet. Cut out the shapes.

2. Make a cut beside each big toe, like this.

3. Cut four pieces of ribbon. Slot them between the toes.

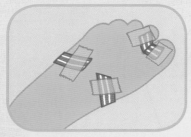

4. Wrap the ribbon around the sides of each foot. Tape the ends onto the back.

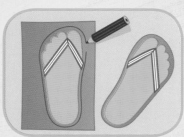

5. Glue the feet onto another piece of paper. Draw around each foot and cut them out.

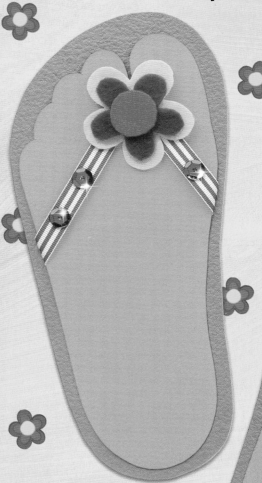

These flowers were cut from felt and glued on.

You could add sequins for decoration.

Animals

Painted lion

For a lioness,
don't paint the
mane in step 3.

Let the
paint
dry
again.

1. **Paint a big
yellow oval for
a lion's body on
some paper.**

2. **Then, paint
four Short legs
at the bottom.
Let it dry.**

3. **Dip a dry brush
into orange paint.
Go around and
around for a mane.**

4. Paint a yellow oval for the face. Then, add two little ears.

5. Paint an orange nose and a shape for the end of the lion's tail.

6. When the paint is dry, use pencils to draw a tail, eyes, a mouth and claws.

Collage crocodile

Use green paint.

1. Paint a piece of thick paper and let it dry.

You could paint a river for your crocodiles to swim in.

Leave space on the paper to draw the head.

2. Draw a shape for a body, and two little feet, on the back of the paper.

The bump is for the eye.

3. Draw a rectangular head. Add a bump on top and zigzag teeth.

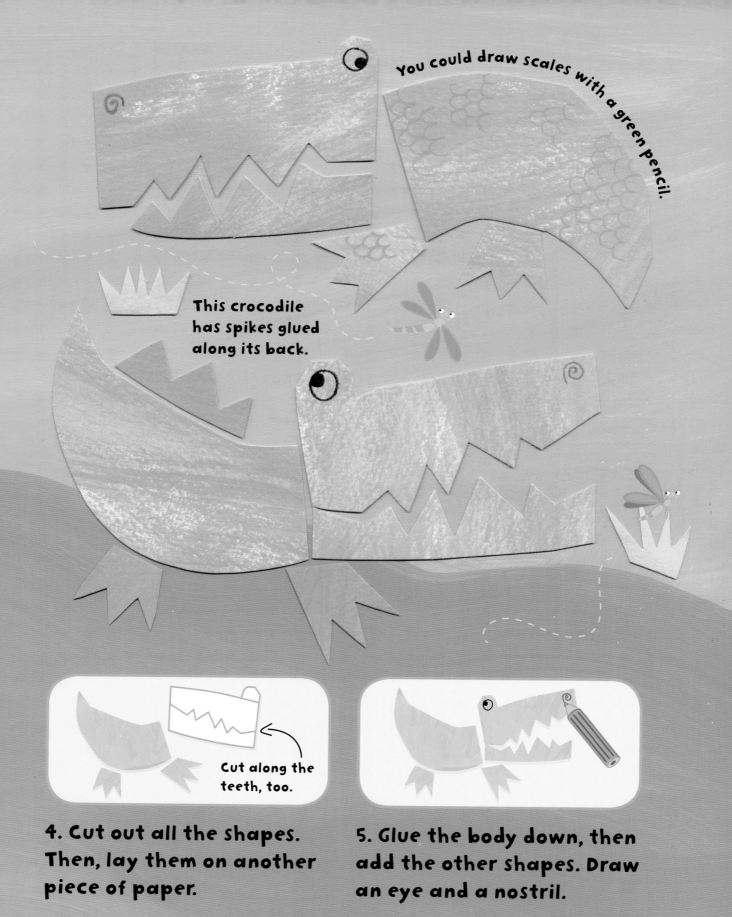

You could draw scales with a green pencil.

This crocodile has spikes glued along its back.

Cut along the teeth, too.

4. Cut out all the shapes. Then, lay them on another piece of paper.

5. Glue the body down, then add the other shapes. Draw an eye and a nostril.

Printed parrot

1. Paint a shape for a parrot's body on a piece of thick paper using blue paint. Then, let it dry.

2. Paint feet, a beak and a pink spot on the cheek. Draw a dot for an eye.

3. Paint three red feathers for the parrot's tail. Add a curly feather on the head, too.

4. Spread dark blue paint on an old plate. Press your hand into it, then print a wing.

5. Press your hand into the paint again and print another wing.

You could paint a branch for your parrot to perch on.

103

Printed giraffe

Use thick paint.

Paint two little horns and a tail, too.

Paint the tip of the horns.

1. Paint a small rectangle for a body. Add a very long neck.

2. Paint a head, ears and four short legs with a thin brush.

3. Paint an orange nose. Add brown hooves, horns and the end of the tail.

4. Spread orange paint on an old plate. Cut a small square of sponge.

5. Dip the sponge in the paint and print shapes on the body and neck.

6. When the paint is dry, draw eyes, a nostril and a mouth.

Stand-up elephant

Don't cut along the fold.

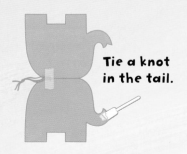

Tie a knot in the tail.

1. Fold a piece of thick paper in half. Draw a body against the fold. Add a trunk, too.

2. Cut around the elephant carefully. Then, open it out and lay it flat.

3. Tape on pieces of thread for a tail. Then, spread glue on the end of the trunk.

You could make an elephant from patterned paper.

Pull the legs apart a little to make the elephant stand up.

Leave the glue to dry.

Glue this part.

4. Fold the elephant in half again, then press the ends of the trunk together.

5. Cut two ears from patterned paper. Fold the side of each ear and glue it.

6. Glue the ears on either side of the body. Then, glue on old buttons for eyes.

Spotted leopard

1. Dip a finger into yellow paint. Fingerpaint a body.

2. Fingerpaint a head and four legs. Add a long tail, too.

You could fingerpaint a plant below your leopard.

Leave the
paint to dry.

3. Fingerprint two yellow dots for ears. Add a brown dot for a nose.

4. Print orange spots all over the leopard. Then, print little brown dots on top.

6. Use pens to draw eyes, a mouth, whiskers and claws.

Striped zebra

Make some of the lines thick and others thin.

1. Paint black stripes on a piece of thick white paper. Let the paint dry.

2. Cut a rectangle for a body from the striped paper. Then, glue it onto some paper.

3. Cut a shape for a neck and one for a head. Glue them onto the body.

4. Cut out ears, legs and a little tail, and glue them on, too.

5. Cut a shape for a nose from pink paper and glue it onto the head.

6. Use pencils to draw a face. Add lines for a hairy mane and tail.

You could cut out
grass from bright,
striped paper.

Fuzzy monkeys

Use pencils to draw vines for your monkey to hang from.

You could cut out leaves from green felt and glue them around your monkey.

Glue the pieces like this.

1. Cut a head and a small body from felt and glue them onto some paper.

2. Cut out an oval for the face and two little ears from paler felt.

3. Glue the face onto the head. Then, glue the ears on either side.

If you don't have felt, you could make a monkey from paper.

4. Use a crayon to draw curving arms and legs. Add fingers and feet.

5. Draw eyes and a mouth. Then, add pink nostrils and cheeks.

6. Bend a fuzzy pipe cleaner to make a tail. Glue it onto the paper.

Happy hippo

Spread the paint on an old plate.

1. Cut the corners off a sponge. Then, cut a small piece out of one side, too.

2. Dip the sponge into some paint and press it onto some paper for the hippo's body.

3. Dip the sponge into the paint again and use it to print a head, like this.

Draw a pink cheek, too.

4. Cut a small rectangle for the legs from another sponge. Dip it into the paint.

5. Print four legs. Then, use your finger to print two little ears. Leave it to dry.

6. Use pens to draw eyes, nostrils and a mouth. Add square teeth with a white pencil.

You could paint a
river and print a
hippo on top when
the paint is dry.

For a swimming hippo, don't
print the legs in step 5.

115

Hairy bear

1. Mix thick brown paint with lots of white glue in an old container.

Paint a light brown snout, too.

2. Paint an oval for a body. Then, add a head, tail and ears.

3. Paint three legs (the fourth one is hidden behind the bear's body).

You could cut fish from foil and glue them onto your picture.

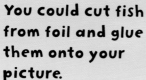

Use the other end of your paintbrush.

4. While the paint is still wet, scratch lots of little lines.

5. When the paint is dry, draw eyes, a nose, a mouth and little brown claws.

You could paint a bear on a rock in a river.

Paper penguin

You could draw a fish
on blue paper.

Draw the shape against the fold.

1. Fold a piece of thick black paper in half. Draw a shape for a body.

2. Draw a line at the top for the penguin's beak, like this.

3. Draw a wing halfway down. Add a flipper below, like this.

Cut along the line shown in yellow.

4. Keeping the paper folded, carefully cut around the shape.

Draw the eyes wide apart.

5. Open out the paper and lay it flat. Use pencils to draw two eyes.

6. Draw a line for the tummy, then fill it in. Fill in the flippers, too.

7. Turn the shape over and use an orange pencil to fill in the beak.

8. Fold the beak down and the flippers up. Fold the wings forward.

9. Crease the middle fold again and stand up your penguin.

Wriggly snakes

Use different chalks.

1. Using the side of a piece of chalk, draw a wavy line. Draw a point at one end.

2. Draw an oval head at the flat end. Then, smudge the snake a little with a finger.

3. Draw patterns on the body. Add dots for eyes and two lines for a forked tongue.

You could draw snakes curling around each other.

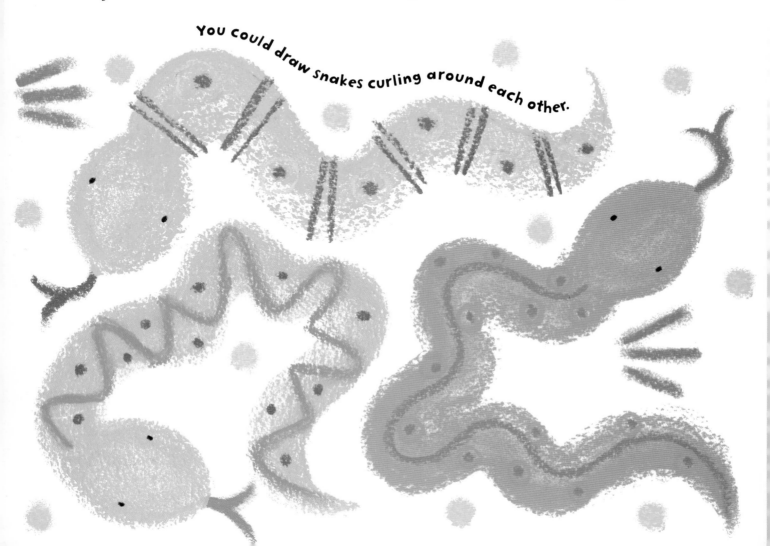

Christmas

Stencil trees

You could print a tree on the front of a Christmas card.

The tree above has lots of overlapping fingerprints.

You don't need this piece.

Use tape to hold the paper.

1. Fold a piece of paper in half. Draw a shape against the fold, like this.

2. Keeping the paper folded, carefully cut out the shape.

3. Open out the paper and lay it flat on a piece of thick paper.

This tree was printed with a sponge, then the wet paint was sprinkled with glitter.

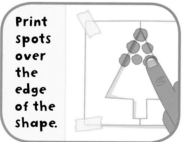

Print spots over the edge of the shape.

4. Dip a finger into paint, then print lots of spots inside the shape.

5. When the paint is dry, lift off the paper. Dab glue onto each spot.

Glue a star on the top ot the tree, too.

6. Press a sequin onto each dot of glue, or sprinkle them with glitter.

Snowman

You could use two cotton cleansing pads.

1. Cut two circles from white felt and glue them onto some paper.

2. Cut a hat from patterned paper or fabric and glue it on, too.

3. Cut a carrot nose from orange felt or paper, and glue it on.

The balls are for the eyes and mouth.

4. Tear tiny pieces of tissue paper and roll them into balls.

5. Glue the balls onto the head. Roll some bigger balls for buttons.

6. Glue the buttons onto the body, then glue on twigs for arms.

You could paint a white hill and glue a snowman on top.

If you don't have any twigs, cut up straws instead.

125

Snowy village

Use a pencil.

1. Draw a hill across a big piece of dark paper.

2. Cut a small square for a house from bright paper.

3. Cut a triangle from pink paper for a roof. Then, draw looping lines across it.

4. Glue the house and roof onto the hill. Cut a small door and glue it on, too.

Use different
papers to make
the houses.

Draw lines
for panes
on each
window.

5. Cut three windows from
yellow paper and glue
them onto the house.

Add dots for snow in the sky, too.

6. Make lots more houses in
the same way. Then, fill in
the hill with white chalk.

Stand-up Santa

Don't cut along the fold.

1. Fold a piece of thick red paper in half. Draw a triangle, like this, and cut it out.

Lay the shape flat.

2. Unfold the shape. Then, draw a line for a hat and a curve for a face.

3. Draw Santa's eyes on either side of the fold. Then, fill in the face with pencils.

Cut along the lines shown in blue.

4. Fold Santa in half again. Cut a shape like this for a nose. Unfold the shape again.

5. Cut two gloves from black paper and glue them onto the body, like this.

Glue the beard under the nose.

6. Pull cotton balls into pieces. Glue two pieces onto the hat and add a long beard.

You could tape a piece
of thread to the back
of the hat to make a
hanging decoration.

You could add
some boots cut
from paper.

Santa's sleigh

Print the reindeer near the sleigh.

1. For Santa's sleigh, fingerprint four shapes onto a piece of paper, like this.

2. Then, do a red fingerprint for his body, and a pink one for his face.

3. For a reindeer, do two brown prints and a red dot for a nose. Let the paint dry.

Draw a line with a blue chalk for a track in the snow. Smudge it a little with a finger.

Add a boot, too.

4. Use pens to draw Santa's arms and legs. Add a hat, beard, face, belt and a glove.

5. Draw antlers, legs and an ear on the reindeer. Add its face, a tail and a collar.

6. Draw the runner on the bottom of the sleigh. Then, add a long rein.

You could add more reindeer pulling Santa's sleigh.

Fingerprint Santa's elves and a snowman, too.

Angels

You could put an angel on the top of a Christmas tree, too.

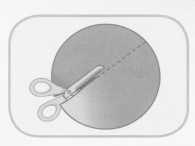

1. Draw around a plate on a piece of paper. Cut out the circle, then cut it in half.

This is for the wings.

2. Spread one of the pieces with glue. Sprinkle it with glitter and leave it to dry.

This will be the dress.

3. Fingerprint dots of glue around the edge of the other piece. Sprinkle them with glitter.

4. Draw a head and face on a small piece of paper. Cut pieces of yarn for hair.

5. Spread glue around the face then press the yarn onto it. Let the glue dry.

6. Then, cut around the face taking care not to cut the strands of hair.

Glue the face on the front of the cone.

7. Bend the dress around to make a cone and tape it together. Glue the face on, too.

Keep the paper folded.

8. Fold the piece for the wings in half. Draw a wing against the fold and cut around it.

9. Unfold the wings. Then, tape them onto the back of the dress, like this.

133

Glittery trees

Keep the cardboard folded.

1. Brush thick paint over a piece of thin cardboard and leave it to dry.

2. Fold the cardboard in half. Then, draw a shape like this, against the fold.

3. Cut along the line. Then, open the tree and lay it flat, with its painted side up.

4. Roll some small pieces of tissue paper into little balls.

134

You could make several trees of different sizes.

Let the glue dry.

5. Then, spread a little glue and some glitter on an old plate.

6. Gently roll each ball in the glue, then roll it in the glitter.

7. Glue on the balls. Add some dots of glue and sprinkle them with glitter.

Finger puppets

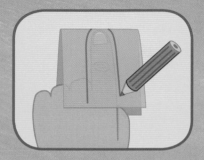

Cut along the line shown in yellow.

Press the arms together.

1. Fold a small piece of paper in half. Then, push a finger up to the fold and draw around it.

2. Draw shapes for arms, then cut out the shape. Don't cut the fold.

3. Unfold the paper. Spread glue on the arms only, then fold the paper again.

Add a felt beard and a crown.

You could bend the arms of the puppet forward.

You could add some sequins, too.

4. Draw a face on another piece of paper, cut it out and glue it on.

Use the same idea to make other puppets.

5. Use pens or paper to add hair. Then, decorate the puppet with shiny paper.

An angel

6. Cut a small piece of paper for a present and glue it on, too.

Mary and baby Jesus

A shepherd

Felt decorations

1. Cut two small squares of felt. Draw a star. Cut it out through both layers.

2. Cut a piece of bright thread. Bend it into a loop, then tie a knot in it.

Leave the loop sticking out for hanging.

3. Spread white glue over one of the star shapes. Lay the ends of the loop on top.

You could thread the loop through a button instead of a bead.

You could use these ideas to make lots of different decorations.

4. Carefully lay the other star on top. Press the shapes together. Let the glue dry.

5. Decorate the star on both sides by gluing on a smaller felt star and sequins.

6. Thread a bead onto the loop, like this. Then, hang up your decoration.

Gift tags

You could use this idea to make Christmas cards, too.

Glue on sequins for extra sparkle.

Use a hole puncher to make the hole.

1. Cut a shape like this from thick paper. Punch a hole near the top.

2. Cut a small strip of cardboard. Then, mix white paint with glue.

3. Dip one edge of the strip into the paint and print a line on the tag.

Use a short strip
to print branches
on a tree.

You could print dots
using the corner of
the cardboard.

Leave it
to dry.

4. Dip the strip
into the paint
again and print
two more lines.

5. Sprinkle the wet
paint with glitter,
then shake off
any excess.

6. Loop some
thread or thin
ribbon through
the hole.

You could decorate a stocking with sequins and more shapes cut from felt.

Stocking

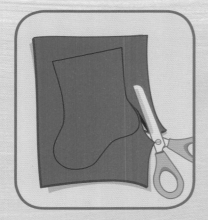

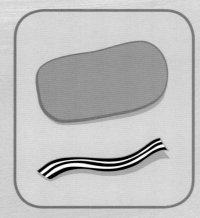

You could glue on pieces of ribbon, too.

1. Draw a large stocking like this on a piece of red felt. Then, cut around it.

2. Cut a band for the top of the stocking, and a piece of ribbon for a loop.

3. Then, cut some presents from cardboard and decorate them with paints.

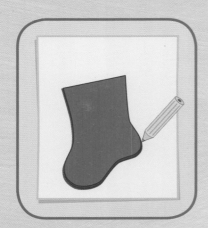

Glue on the band last of all.

4. Lay the stocking on a piece of thin cardboard and draw around it.

5. Spread glue inside the shape. Scrunch up tissue paper and press it on.

6. Glue the presents and the ribbon at the top. Then, glue on the red stocking.

You could glue on sequins for extra sparkle.

Snowflakes

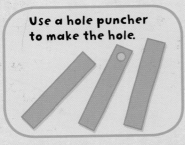

Use a hole puncher to make the hole.

1. Cut three strips of cardboard. Then, punch a hole in the end of one.

Sprinkle one side with glitter while the paint is wet.

2. Mix thick white paint with glue, then paint the strips on both sides.

3. Lay the strips on top of one another, like this, then glue them together.

4. When the glue is dry, wrap thick thread around the snowflake.

5. Secure the thread with a knot. Loop thread through the hole for hanging.

144